Raising the Stakes

All In Book 2

Lacey Cross

Contents

Chapter 1

Three days since I let Tony bend me over his desk.

Three days of my husband finding excuses to touch my throat, his fingers brushing my collarbone where the hickey Tony gave me is fading. Robert's been watching me across rooms with a new kind of hunger. Not the comfortable desire of fifteen years of marriage—this is something rawer. When I reach for my coffee mug at breakfast, his gaze locks on my hand and I know he's picturing them gripping the edge of Tony's desk. When I turn my back to him in the kitchen, I feel his stare drag down my spine like he's visualizing exactly what Tony did to me.

At dinner last night, I was mid-sentence about the Wellington Foundation's spring fundraiser when I caught him staring at my mouth. He was watching my lips move, and I knew exactly what he was imagining. Me on my knees... begging.

The clawing need deep in my belly hasn't quieted since that night at the casino. I want more, but I don't want this to ruin our marriage.

The hickey's almost gone. The yellow-green shadow isn't visible unless you knew it was there. But Robert knows where to look.

I'm lying against his chest, his heartbeat steady under my cheek. It's after midnight and we should be sleeping, but his thumb keeps stroking the fading bruise. The touch is soothing and hypnotic. My thoughts drift, softening at the edges.

"Shannon."

I press my cheek harder into his chest. "Mmm?"

"The casino."

Just two words, but they land like stones. I'm immediately awake and my shoulders tense. I've been waiting for this. Dreading it. Craving it so badly I can barely breathe.

"What about it?" I attempt nonchalance and fail.

His thumb stops.

"You know what I mean."

Yeah. I know. That's the problem. We've been pretending everything was normal for three days. We drank our coffee in the morning while he scrolled through emails and I took a charity committee call for the Wellington Foundation that I don't remember agreeing to. We had dinners at our usual spots, both pretending nothing had changed.

Totally normal.

Except Robert kept staring at my neck. And every night he fucked me harder than usual and asked me filthy questions.

Did it feel like this?

Was he rough with you?

Tell me. Tell me what he did. Tell me again.

I told him. Over and over. And every time, something settled into his expression. Not jealousy. Not anger.

Lust.

He caresses my neck again, thumb brushing my collarbone. We can't avoid the conversation any longer.

He speaks before I do. "I want you to go back."

Holy shit. He said it.

"Robert—"

"I haven't thought about anything else. Three days straight." His laugh is short and surprised. "I didn't know it would feel like this."

I push up on my elbow so I can see him. His silver hair is mussed and stubble shadows his jaw. But even though it's late, he looks energized in a way I haven't seen in years.

Even though his meaning is clear, I need him to spell it out. "You're sure you want me to go back?"

"Yes."

"And do what?"

He brushes his finger along my bottom lip. "Whatever you want to do."

My stomach flips. Part of me hoped he'd say this, but another part hoped he'd come to his senses these last few days and forbid it. It would have been easier if he told me I was only his.

I know how to be told no. I've been told no my whole life—by my mother, by society, by the good-girl voice in my head.

If he'd forbidden it, I could blame him. Be the good wife who craved something she couldn't have.

But permission? This means it's my choice.

"What if I don't want to?"

"Then don't."

"You wouldn't be disappointed?"

"I'd be disappointed if you did something just for me and lied to me." He caresses my cheek. "So don't lie. What do you actually want?"

Silence.

I could make a joke about being too old for this. Too tired. Too whatever. But Robert's patient eyes are unraveling me.

Fuck it. I'm tired of hiding.

"I want to go back." The truth tumbles out. "I want... what I had in that office. Someone looking at me like—"

I stop. Try again. "Like I'm actually there. Not just... an ornament at another fucking charity gala."

My throat tightens. I swallow hard.

"I want to be more than... than this house and those fucking committees and—" I can't finish. I didn't mean to say that much.

"What else?"

"I don't know." Snuggling closer, I tuck my head against his shoulder. "I want to know if that woman at the casino was really me or just—I don't know..."

I've thought about this, but I'm not sure how to explain it.

"Say it." His voice is quiet but firm.

God.

I search for the words. "I want to feel powerful. But also—I don't know—not powerful? At the same time. Does that sound insane?"

Silence.

But I'm not done. "I want to choose it. When I give in. Who I give in to." The words come out quieter. "And I don't know if that's fucked up or—"

Jesus. Listen to me. Who even says that out loud?

"I want it so much it scares me."

Robert strokes my back for a long moment before speaking. "You want to know what I was thinking? That whole night you were gone?"

"What?"

"I was thinking about you walking into that casino in your gala dress. All those men watching you. Wanting you." His voice goes rough. "I was thinking about what you'd do with them."

My thighs press together, slick heat building from nothing but his words.

"Robert—"

"When you texted me to tell me that you were stopping at the casino..." He groans. "I got so damn hard." His lips brush my ear. "And when you came home with his cum inside you... fuck, I almost lost my mind."

"In a good way?"

When he speaks, his voice drops lower. "In the way that makes me want to hear you say his name while I'm fucking you."

Holy shit, that's filthy.

His gaze is dark. Intense. "Watching you come while you told me about him was the hottest thing I've ever experienced. I still want what I said originally. You have permission to have fun and then come home and tell me everything."

Oh thank god. I didn't know how much I needed to hear that until he said it.

"What if it changes things?"

"It already has." Robert cups my jaw. "I want you to be the woman you were in that office."

"She might be a lot."

"I'm counting on it." His thumb drags along my lower lip, and something raw flashes in his eyes. "I want to see what she does."

Something breaks open in my chest, relief or arousal or maybe both—I can't tell anymore.

"Saturday," I whisper. I slide my hand up his chest, feeling his heartbeat quicken under my palm. "I'll go back Saturday."

"Yeah?"

"Yeah. I'll go back and see what trouble I can get into."

His kiss is bruising. Possessive. When he breaks away, we're both breathing hard.

"I want every detail," he says. "Every dirty thing you do."

Lust spreads low in my body, but underneath it, I'm apprehensive. I just hope this doesn't fuck everything up and ruin what we've built over fifteen years.

Chapter 2

By the time Saturday rolls around, I'm a wet mess from daydreaming about fucking Tony again.

Robert and I are having our morning coffee at the kitchen table when he pauses and then sets his mug down. I can tell he means business.

"Okay. If we're doing this, we need parameters. Clear ones. For both of us."

I laugh nervously and side-eye him. "Parameters? Really?" God, he's being so thoughtful about this while all I can think about is Tony's hands on me.

"I need to know you're safe."

I take his hand and squeeze it. "Fine. What parameters?"

"You text me when you leave."

"Okay."

"You tell me everything afterward. Every detail." His voice drops. "I want to know what he does to you. How he touches you. What he says. I want to hear all of it."

Heat crawls up my chest. I shift on the chair. The seam of my robe drags against sensitive skin.

"You sure?"

"Everything." His eyes lock on mine. "I want to hear how much of a slut my wife is when I'm not around."

The word slut makes my nipples tighten. I want him to say it again.

"What else?"

His voice softens. "No feelings. This is just physical. And at the end of the night, at the end of every night—"

"I come home to you."

"Always." The word is fierce. "You can fuck whomever you want. Let them do whatever you want. But you're always mine."

I lift his fingers to my lips. Press a kiss to his knuckles.

"Always."

His smile is wolfish, and I glance at the bulge in his sweat-pants.

"Robert." I laugh. "Wait—are you seriously hard right now?"

"Are you seriously asking? We're talking about you fuck-ing other men while I sit at home thinking about it. And you're surprised?"

"I guess I—" I lose the thought as he stands and pulls me out of my chair. His erection presses into my hip. "Oh."

"Yeah. Oh." He kisses my neck. "Every time I think about another man's hands on you—" He bites down. Not too rough, but enough to make me gasp. "I want to fuck you until you forget your own name and then send you out to let someone else try the same thing."

"That's a little twisted."

He slides a hand under my robe and cups my breast. "Is that a problem?"

"No," I moan as he plays with my nipple. "Not a problem."

He skims his hand down my body and between my legs. His groan vibrates through me. "You're drenched. My filthy wife."

"Robert—"

Two fingers push inside me and I clench around them, craving more.

"Look at me," he commands.

His face is inches from mine, gray eyes burning. I struggle to focus as he finger fucks me.

"When you're there"—he drives deep—"I want you to think"—another hard thrust—"about how hard I'm going to fuck you"—he slams into me—"after he's done with you."

"Yes." I can barely get the word out. "Yes."

The orgasm is building, coiling tight. But right before I explode, he withdraws his fingers.

I whimper, "Wait."

"Gotta keep your pussy needy until later."

Ugh. I press my forehead to his shoulder and try to catch my breath.

"You suck," I manage, but there's no malice in the words.

He laughs, low and satisfied. "No, but maybe you will tonight."

I give him a dirty look as he helps me straighten my robe. I like this new side to my husband, even if it didn't get me an orgasm. Hopefully "later" will be worth the wait.

I'm standing in my walk-in closet, staring at the green dress laid across the ottoman. It's tight and short, the kind of thing I'd never wear to a charity function. It's perfect for the casino.

This time, I'm not improvising in a parking lot with make-up and shaking hands. This time, I'm picking out my dress in advance and hopefully going to get good and well fucked tonight.

The dress clings as I put it on, and the neckline dips lower than I'd normally risk. I pair it with spiked black heels. My calves will hate me later. I don't care.

Smoky eyes, dark red lips. The woman in the mirror looks like a stranger.

Last time I looked like this, I didn't know what was about to happen.

Tonight I do.

"You look sinful."

I turn. Robert's leaning in the doorway, arms crossed, watching me with a possessive gleam.

"That's the idea." I reach for my clutch. It's just big enough for my phone, cash, and the wedding ring I'll take off before I walk into the casino.

"Come here."

I cross to him. He pulls me close, one hand sliding into my hair, the other gripping my hip hard enough to remind me who I belong to.

"Have fun." He kisses me—deep and claiming, the kind that wrecks my lipstick and makes me forget I'm supposed to leave. "Come back broke."

I blink at him, then can't help the delighted laugh that escapes. "You're insane."

His lips brush my ear. "Penniless and needy. That's how I want you tonight."

"Okay." I laugh again and pull away. If I have my way, I'll come back thoroughly fucked and anything but needy.

The Goldpoint Casino glows red and gold against the dark sky. Neon sign blinking JACKPOT JACKPOT JACK-POT.

I park and sit in the car. Count my heartbeats.

One... two... three...

Holy fuck. Am I really doing this again?

Twelve... thirteen... fourteen...

Last time I was here, I was reckless and craving a thrill I couldn't name.

Twenty-two...

Tonight is different.

Tonight, I'm walking in with my eyes wide open.

When I count fifty, I grab my clutch and twist off my wedding ring. I haven't even gotten into the casino yet and there are already so many numbers. Fifty heartbeats, three carats, fifteen years. At our wedding, I'm not sure whose hands shook more—Robert's when he slipped it on, or mine when I felt the weight. They're steady now.

As I tuck the ring into my clutch, my phone buzzes.

ROBERT: I'm already thinking about later. Tell me everything.

I smile as I type.

SHANNON: I will. I promise.

ROBERT: Go get what you want.

I send him a kiss emoji and put my phone in my clutch.

Should I feel guilty? I used to believe good wives didn't do things like this. That version of me is quiet tonight.

When I get out of the car, the cool night air slides over my bare legs. Goosebumps dot my thighs and exposed shoulders. I smooth my dress and check my reflection in the car window. The woman staring back at me looks ready for anything.

I chose this.

My heels click against the pavement. The glass doors slide open and the noise hits me first.

Laughter from somewhere near the craps tables. Cards shuffling, chips clicking together. A hundred conversations blending into one low roar.

I feel powerful and sexy as I stroll in. The heels add four inches to my height and a dangerous angle to my walk. A man at a table does a double take. A security guard's attention snags on my legs and lingers there.

Good.

I bypass the poker room and head to the bar for a drink instead. I need to think. How do I get Tony's attention? Is he even working tonight? Shit, I didn't consider that. But it's Saturday—the manager should be here.

The bar is tucked into a corner near the main floor. I slide onto a stool.

"You're back." The bartender is in her late thirties with a sleeve tattoo on her forearm—roses and thorns. Her dark hair is pulled back.

I don't remember seeing her last time, and I would have. My pulse jumps. "You know me?"

"I remember faces." She picks up a clean glass and polishes it anyway. "Especially faces Tony asks about."

Heat floods through me. "Tony asked about me?"

"The brunette in the red dress who couldn't pay her tab." A knowing smile. "I'm supposed to tell him if you come back in. He doesn't usually ask about anyone."

My hands are shaking and I don't know what to do with them, so I press them flat against my thighs.

"Is that good or bad?"

"Depends." She sets down the glass and leans forward on her elbows. "You're not in trouble, are you?"

She's looking at me with an assessing gaze, and I'm suddenly curious what happens to people in trouble.

"I'm here because I want to be."

"Good." She straightens up. "What're you drinking?"

"Whiskey. Neat."

Not my usual. Mrs. Robert Matthews drinks Chardonnay at charity galas and martinis at dinner parties.

But whoever this Shannon is becoming? She drinks whiskey in bars while powerful men ask about her.

The bartender pours generously and she pushes it toward me.

"I'm Diana."

"Shannon."

"I know." She grins. "Like I said. Tony asked."

I wrap my fingers around the glass, but before I take a sip, a hand touches my elbow.

It's a young guy in a casino security vest who hardly looks old enough to work here. There's a nervous energy surrounding him like he's delivering a message he doesn't fully understand.

"Ma'am? Mr. Ricci would like to see you."

My heart slams against my ribs.

Diana's watching me, amusement in her eyes. "Go on." She tips her chin toward the rear of the casino. "Don't keep him waiting."

I leave the whiskey untouched on the bar.

CHAPTER 3

Same elevator. Same hallway. Same plush carpet muffling my heels. Same brass nameplate on the door at the end: Antonio Ricci—Private.

But I'm not the same.

Last time, I stumbled down this hallway in a fog of desperation. Barely knowing what I wanted. Terrified of what I might find.

Tonight I'm walking with purpose. Shoulders squared. Chin up.

I know what's behind that door, and I want it.

I knock.

"Come in."

His voice lands somewhere low in my body, and I can feel my panties growing damp.

I push open the door.

Tony's behind his desk. Wearing a black polo, sleeves straining against his muscular arms. That expensive watch on his wrist. Silver threading through his dark hair at the temples.

Same skyline through the floor-to-ceiling windows behind him. Same photo on the wall—Tony with the senator-looking guy.

He doesn't smile when he sees me, just looks me over, slowly.

"You came back."

"Yes."

He stands and moves around the desk toward me. When he stops a foot away, he's close enough that I can smell the woodsy pine of his cologne. Close enough that I have to tilt my head to meet his gaze.

My mouth goes dry and my breasts ache. My body knows what I'm here for.

"You dressed up." His attention drops to my cleavage. "For me?"

"Maybe I dressed up for myself."

He laughs. "I like that." His fingers come up, brushing my jaw. "If you came back, that only means one thing."

My breath catches at his touch, and I lean into it. Getting him to fuck me is going to be easier than I expected, but something inside me rebels at being so transparent.

"I could be here to gamble."

"I'm just saving you the hassle of having to lose money to get fucked."

He smirks, and I wish it wasn't true. I just want him to bend me over his desk again and call me filthy names. If he spanked me again, I'd just beg for more.

"My mark faded." His thumb skims my collarbone where his mark used to be. I notice a thin scar across the ridge of his knuckles. A story I don't know, and probably never will. "I'll have to fix that."

"Tony—"

"Unless you really did come here to gamble tonight." He circles and stops behind me, his breath warm on my skin. "Does the slut wife want to run up another tab she can't pay?"

The fiction. The game we're playing. He thinks I'm pretending to be wealthy when really I'm pretending to be poor.

"Depends on what happens afterwards." My words come out breathy.

His palms land on my hips. Hard enough that I'll have bruises tomorrow. New marks to show Robert. "The real question is what're you willing to bet."

He pulls me against him. His stiff cock presses into my ass through his slacks, and I fight to hold in a moan. God, I'm dripping from nothing but his hands on me. Why do I want this so bad?

"What's the stake?"

"Everything." His mouth finds my neck. Teeth scrape skin. "I want you to walk out of here owing me so much you'll spend weeks paying it off with your pussy."

Mmm, why is this so hot?

His fingers curl possessively around my waist. "I have your panties from last time in my desk drawer. I knew you'd be back."

Holy fuck. My panties. What's he been doing with them since then? The thought makes me dizzy.

His hand slides along my thigh and up under my dress. He presses his cock harder against my ass as his fingers brush the silk of my panties.

"You're drenched." There's satisfaction in his tone. "You walked in here dripping for me."

"Yes."

"Say it louder."

"Yes," I cry out as my head falls against his shoulder and my clutch slips from my fingers and tumbles to the floor. "I've been thinking about this all week. About what you did to me."

"Tell me." His fingers slide under my panties and between my wet folds. I shiver in pleasure as he rubs my clit. "What have you been thinking about?"

"Your hands. Your mouth." I'm panting now and rocking against him. "You fucking me on your desk."

"Good girl." The words hit me like electricity. "Keep talking."

"I thought about it at dinner with my husband. On the phone. Lying in bed at three in the morning pretending to be asleep."

He speeds up his fingers, and I gasp and rush out, "I touched myself thinking about you."

"Fuck." His hold on my hip tightens. "You're a hungry little slut who can't stop thinking about my cock."

There's a knock at the door, and I jump.

Tony's fingers go motionless between my thighs, and he growls, "Not now."

The door opens anyway.

I freeze. For one sick second, I imagine being caught. Exposed. Dragged out of here and then seeing it splashed all over the media. Rich wife fucks casino manager behind her husband's back—but no, Tony's running this. I'm safe.

And the fear curdles into an illicit thrill so strong that it's impossible to think of anything beyond this moment.

"Sorry." The newcomer's tone is deep and male. He doesn't sound sorry at all. "I didn't realize you had company."

He moves into my line of sight. The guy is in his mid-thirties and wearing an expensive charcoal suit. Tall, dark-haired, with sharp features that make him intimidating. He's not smiling.

His attention moves from Tony to me. To where Tony's hand is under my dress. A flush creeps up my neck. There's no way this isn't what it looks like.

The guy's expression is locked down tight, with no emotion. Does he walk in on his boss fingering women often?

"This is Adrian," Tony says dryly. "My business partner."

Adrian.

He looks me over slowly. He's colder than Tony. Calculating.

"This the one from last weekend?"

Tony told him about me. Probably told him he fucked some desperate slut who needed to pay off her debt.

I brace for a wave of humiliation.

It doesn't come. Instead heat flares deep in my core, white-hot and obliterating. The world narrows to the ache between my legs. I'm a desperate slut, and it's glorious.

Before the casino, I was invisible at a charity gala. Now two men are standing here, one with his hand against my pussy, and I—what was I thinking? It's gone.

I rock my hips, and Tony chuckles before withdrawing his fingers slowly. He makes sure Adrian sees what he's been doing.

I shudder at the loss of contact and whimper.

"She's my guest." Tony moves to stand beside me, one palm resting possessively on the small of my spine.

"Sure." Adrian doesn't sound convinced. "The shipment's been delayed. We need to talk about the alternative supplier."

"Now?"

"Unless you want to explain to Hendricks why his delivery is three days late."

A silent conversation passes between them. One I can't read. Tony's jaw tightens, but he nods.

"Fine. Make it quick."

Adrian moves to the bar cart and pours himself two fingers of whiskey. He talks without looking at Tony. Running through numbers and names and logistics that sound like more than casino operations.

Suppliers. Payments. Someone named Hendricks who doesn't like to wait. A secondary account for the overflow. Contacts who need to be handled before the next shipment. Deliveries and accounts and scheduling conflicts.

I stand frozen by the desk, trying to follow the conversation and failing. The words are ordinary enough, but there's an underlying current that makes the hair on the back of my neck stand up.

Tony's photo with the state senator. The way staff straighten when he walks through the casino. The expensive watch.

What the fuck have I stumbled into? And should I be hearing all of this?

Adrian finishes his drink. Sets down the glass. Finally turns to look at me.

"You think you know what you're playing at." His tone is soft. Almost kind. The contrast with his flat expression makes it worse. It sounds like he's seen women like me before, and it didn't end well for them.

"She knows how to handle her debts." Tony's palm presses harder against my spine. "Don't you, Shannon?"

"Yes." My voice is thin and breathless, and for one small moment I wonder if giving him my real first name last time was a smart choice. Suppliers. Shipments. Secondary accounts. The words circle back, clicking into place like tumblers in a lock. Christ, why didn't I use a fake name?

Adrian holds my gaze for one more beat before nodding to Tony and walking out. The door closes behind him with a soft click.

Silence.

I stand frozen, trying to name the sensation crawling up my spine. Fear? Excitement? Both?

Then Tony laughs, short and harsh. "I think he liked you. He's not usually that chatty."

"I'm not so sure of that." That was him liking someone? I'd hate to see what happens if he doesn't.

"Trust me. He was one second away from asking if he could fuck your sweet pussy." He turns me to face him, closing his hands around my upper arms. "If you want him to, I'm sure it could be arranged."

Wait. What?

"Why would I want—"

"Because you do." Tony's gaze is frank. "You weren't embarrassed when he walked in. It excited you."

"That's not—"

"Don't lie to me." His fingers dig in. "If I had fucked you right in front of him, you would have loved it."

I can't breathe because he's right.

The moment Adrian's attention landed on me and found Tony's hand between my thighs, I was so turned on I couldn't think.

"Next time you bet more than you can afford," Tony murmurs, "he might want to collect too."

The way he says it—like Adrian getting his hands on me is a foregone conclusion. Like I'm a prize to be split. My entire body buzzes at the thought of being passed between them.

He releases me and walks around his desk before pausing.

"Shannon, tell me, do you want me to fuck you?"

Why is he asking me this now? Isn't it obvious? He must be able to read the confusion on my face because he continues.

"I need to hear you say it. I don't fuck unwilling women. You can walk out of here and nothing bad will happen. But you have to say what you want."

My clit pulses, and I whisper, "I want you to fuck me. Use me however you want."

Saying that out loud pings that place deep inside of me that wants to be taken and used without having to ask for it, but I also want to own this moment.

He smiles and opens his desk drawer. My eyes grow wide when he pulls out my panties from last time.

They're dangling from his fingers. "Want these back?"

I like the idea of him having them, so I'm not sure what the correct answer is.

When I don't reply, he moves back to me and kisses me hard. His tongue pushes into my mouth. His hands are everywhere, palming my ass, hiking up my dress.

He breaks off the kiss, and before I can even catch my breath, he grabs my chin hard, prying my lips apart. He dangles my week-old panties in front of my face, the fabric stiff from my juices soaking into them. I open my mouth wider, eager for it, and he shoves them right in, stuffing the dirty panties deep into my mouth.

Lust hits me so hard my vision blurs, my pussy clenching with need. The taste explodes on my tongue—salty, musky tang from dried arousal.

God, I've got my nasty, used panties crammed in my mouth, gagging me with my own slutty flavor. This is way filthier than anything I've ever done, and it makes me so fucking wet.

He smirks down at me, his hand still gripping my chin. "Taste that, you little slut? That's your greedy pussy all over those panties. Admit it—tell me how much of a desperate fucktoy you are for my cock."

I mumble around the fabric, the words muffled but clear enough. "I'm such a slut for your cock. I need it so bad, like the fucktoy I am."

He spins me around to face his desk and his voice is rough at my neck. "Can you taste my cum on them? I've been jerking off into them all week."

When he says that, my mouth waters. Yeah, this is even filthier than I realized.

"Bend over."

This is exactly what I came for. I rest my palms flat on the polished wood and as I lean forward, he pushes my shoulder down. I turn my head, resting my cheek on the surface. The Seattle skyline is through the window, and I suddenly get the insane thought that if someone was using a telescope to look into the office, they'd be getting quite the show.

He bunches my dress at my waist and yanks my panties to my knees. I try to hold steady in my heels and realize that could get dangerous. I kick them off, while behind me I hear his belt buckle. The metal clink. Then the rasp of his zipper. Each sound louder than it should be.

"You're going to take everything I give you." His fist tangles in my hair. Pulls my head up.

"Yes," I mumble around my panties.

"And when you go home to your husband tonight, you're going to be thinking about how hard you came on my cock."

My cry is muffled as he drives into me with one hard thrust. My palms slide across the desk and I clutch the edge for stability.

Oh god. Oh fuck.

He's bigger than I remembered. Thicker. The stretch burns and I gasp, trying to relax around him. When he's finally seated, the room goes soft from pleasure.

"That's it." He fucks me in long, punishing strokes that rock me forward with each impact.

I'm squealing and moaning as he pounds me against his desk. I'm being so loud, not even the panties can block it all.

He keeps one fist in my hair and the other digs into my hip hard enough to leave marks.

"This pussy is mine tonight." His tone is ragged now, losing its polish. "Gonna fill you so full, you'll smell like me tomorrow."

All I can do is hold on to the desk as the pleasure builds in layers. Fuuuck, this is amazing.

The desk scrapes against the floor, and I'm barreling towards an enormous orgasm. Each drag of his cock massages every inch of me, and I can't think beyond the growing delight.

I'm being split apart by a man who isn't my husband, and I've never felt more alive.

My thighs tremble as the orgasm builds. There's a deep pressure and I try to slam backwards against his cock in a frenzy.

Tony releases my hair and reaches between my legs, circling my clit as his thrusts turn shorter.

"Come for me." he growls. "Come all over my cock like the hungry little slut you are."

I shatter. The release rolls through me—god—waves—each one stronger. I'm sobbing, the panties mostly muffling the sound. I can't think, can't breathe. My body convulses and Tony doesn't stop. He keeps fucking me through the pleasure, chasing his own orgasm.

When he comes, it's with a groan that vibrates through me. I can taste him on my panties, the salt-musk heat of it, and I know that's what he's pumping into me right now.

The image of Robert pops into my head. Is he stroking himself right now? God, I hope he likes this story.

Tony pulls out slowly and I slump against the desk. I hear fabric rustling as he tugs his clothes back into place.

"Stay there."

I'm too wrecked to move anyway. My cheek is pressed to the cool wood and the whole room is fuzzy.

His fingers follow the inside of my thigh. High. Near my pussy.

"Here." His mouth follows his fingers. There's hot breath against sensitive skin. "Somewhere only he'll see."

He sucks hard enough to sting. Hard enough that I know Robert will press his thumb to this bruise tomorrow and he'll get that look—the one that says 'mine'. Even after all of this.

When Tony pulls away, the throb of his new mark is already blooming.

"Now everyone who matters will know."

I'm a mess when he helps me off the desk. He pulls my panties from my mouth and tucks them into his jeans pocket. He grins. "Yeah, you're not getting these back."

He straightens my clothes and I let him lead me to a chair. He sits me down and retrieves my clutch from the floor before getting me a bottle of water from a tiny fridge.

"Drink. You aren't leaving until I'm sure you can walk straight."

I take a few sips, each one clearing my head more. I can see my reflection in a mirror on the wall. My lipstick is smeared. My hair is wrecked.

I look like a woman who got fucked senseless and isn't sorry about it.

Tony pours himself a whiskey and sits in his office chair, one ankle crossed over his knee. He looks satisfied, like a cat that's finished playing with its prey.

"Adrian thinks you're trouble."

I turn toward him. My brain is finally working again. "What do you think?"

"I think he's right." His mouth curves. "The best kind of trouble."

"Should I be worried? About him?"

"Adrian?" Tony considers. "He doesn't trust anyone. Takes him a while to warm up. But once you're in?" He shrugs. "He's loyal."

"And until then?"

"Until then, he'll watch you. Try to figure out what game you're playing." Tony's gaze glitters. "He's very good at figuring things out."

The hair on my neck stands up. His conversation with Adrian. Suppliers and payments and someone who doesn't like to wait. A secondary account for overflow. Contacts who need to be handled.

I need to tell Robert about that part, and I'm supposed to tell him everything.

The thought rises and I push it down. Not tonight. Tonight I want to give him the good parts. Getting fucked over the desk with my dirty panties in my mouth.

The questions about what Tony and Adrian are really doing here? Those I'll keep.

The first secret I've hidden from my husband.

"Tony. What—"

"Go play some cards." He cuts me off, gentle but firm. "Your credit is good here. Have some fun."

He's done with me. Whatever he and Adrian are involved in, it's better that I don't know.

"Okay." I slide on my heels. "I'll see you."

"You will." Not a question. "And Shannon?"

I pause at the door.

"Next time you're here, make sure you say hello to Adrian. He's going to want to get to know you better."

CHAPTER 4

The elevator deposits me onto the casino floor.

I'm a mess. My thighs are slick. I carry Tony's cologne like a second skin. The new mark on my inner thigh throbs with every step. A secret pulse that only Robert will see.

Heat coils between my legs. I should go home to my husband, but my body isn't ready to leave yet. Plus, Robert told me to come home broke and I have cash burning a hole in my clutch.

The orgasm Tony gave me is humming through my body. Warm and satisfied. But underneath it there's an edge. A new hunger.

A hunger with a name: Adrian.

Tony sees me as a prize he's already won.

Adrian sees me as something to figure out.

I don't know which one makes me wetter.

God, I'm such a slut. I just fucked Tony and I'm already thinking of another guy.

The poker room draws me in. Players hunched over green felt inside. Faces tense with concentration or desperation.

The host is the same as last time, and he just nods with a small smile playing at his lips.

Do all the employees know who I am now? The woman who ran up a tab she couldn't pay. The one Tony asked about.

There's an empty seat at a mid-stakes table. The buy-in is higher than last time. Five hundred minimum.

I buy in and join the game. The other players take in my tousled appearance, and a zing of naughty pleasure makes me smile. Let them look. Let them see the sex-flushed cheeks, the woman who's practically vibrating in her seat.

Tony's cum leaks into my panties. I feel the bruise with every shift.

The first hand is dealt.

By the time I'm done here, I'll owe this place more than money. And that's exactly what I want.

I'm ready for someone to think I can't pay again.

The first hand, I bet too high.

The second hand, I stay in when I know I should fold.

By the third hand, I've stopped thinking about strategy entirely.

The cards blur in front of me. Kings and queens and numbers that used to mean something back in college. Back when I was the girl who always won at poker. Now I'm the woman who gets fucked in casino offices.

I'm not playing to win. I'm playing for orgasms.

Every chip I push into the center is another small surrender. Another way of saying yes to whatever this night wants to give me. The rush of the bet. The sick thrill when I lose. The way my heart kicks knowing I'm throwing away money that could buy plane tickets, mortgage payments, a semester of someone's college tuition.

Mrs. Robert Matthews could never play this recklessly.

Whoever I am tonight absolutely would.

The losses pile up. When my chips run out, more appear in front of me without a word exchanged. I know Tony arranged this. The dealer's expression stays neutral, but I catch the glances between him and the pit boss hovering at the edge of the room. They're watching me spiral. Watching the debt grow. Probably seen it a hundred times. People chasing a high they can't name, bleeding money onto the felt.

I don't stop. Thousands. Gone in less than an hour. I got fucked, yet I'm still craving what I came here for.

I want to owe them more more money than I currently have on me. I think I'm there.

The pit boss approaches. He's polite, professional, his smile not reaching his eyes.

"Ma'am, we'll need to settle up before you continue."

I reach for my clutch. I probably almost have enough cash in there. The ATM can give me the rest. I could end this right now, walk out with nothing but a dent in our savings and a story to tell Robert.

A hand closes around my elbow.

"I'll handle this."

It's Adrian.

His hold is firm, but not painful. The pit boss gives a nod of deference. "Of course, Mr. Cole."

Adrian doesn't acknowledge him. His attention is on me.

"Come with me."

He steers me away from the table, through a door marked STAFF ONLY, down a corridor that smells like industrial cleaner.

We stop at a storage room, and when he opens the door there are metal shelves stacked with boxes. A mop bucket in the corner. The muffled roar of the casino seeps through the thin walls.

This is nothing like Tony's office. No leather. No skyline. No expensive whiskey on a bar cart.

This is utilitarian. A place where things get handled.

Adrian closes the door behind us. His tone is calm. "Do you want to settle your debt?"

I'm so turned on I can barely breathe. Fuck yes, I want to settle it.

My heart slams against my ribs. "I have money. I can pay."

"Is that really what you want?" He moves toward me, and I step backward until my shoulders hit the wall.

"Tony and I have an arrangement—"

"Tony's not here." Adrian stops inches from me. His eyes give me nothing. "I am."

"I want it." Heat floods through me and every inch of me waits for contact.

This. Yes. This is what I hoped for. Maybe not in a storage closet, but sometimes the universe gives you what you need, not what you expect.

"You're still dripping." It's not a question. "Did Tony fuck you that good, or are you that hungry?"

"Both." The word slips out before I can stop it.

His jaw loosens. Like I've passed a test I didn't know I was taking.

"Turn around."

I do.

He yanks my dress up over my ass. "Hands on the wall. Don't move them."

I flatten my palms against cold concrete as I hear the zipper of his slacks. Oh god, I'm really going to get fucked again. It's good Robert said I could do whatever I want.

"You didn't leave." His voice rumbles behind me. "Tony said I'd find you gambling. Said you were the type."

"What type?"

"The type who needs to be treated like a slut. Your husband probably can't fuck you hard enough."

He's wrong. Robert can fuck me hard, but he can't make me feel cheap like this does. I keep the thought to myself and moan as he palms my wet panties.

I hear him exhale. Maybe the first crack in his control. Maybe proof I'm not the only one affected by this.

"You're the type who gets off on being used by men who aren't her husband."

"My husband knows—"

"Does he?" Adrian's fingers push my panties aside. "Does he know you're in a storage room right now, about to get fucked by a man you just met?"

I don't answer. Can't answer because he's right.

Robert knows about Tony. He doesn't know about this. He probably doesn't imagine me pressed against a concrete wall with a stranger's fingers sliding through my pussy lips.

"Does your husband know what a whore he married?"

The word sends a shock through my system, and a ripple of pleasure runs from my fingertips to my toes.

It fits. Fits like something I've been missing without knowing it had a name.

"Yes." My voice comes out wrecked. "He knows. He loves it."

Adrian laughs. Short, humorless. "Then he's just as fucked up as we are, because knowing you're married just makes this hotter."

He drives into me without warning. I cry out. His palm clamps over my mouth. He's thick—so thick—and for a second I hang there. Impaled. Forgetting how to breathe.

"Quiet." His hips move. Hard. "Unless you want the whole casino to hear what a hungry whore you are."

The pace he sets is relentless. Each stroke shoves me into the concrete. His other hand digs crescents into my hip. More marks to bring home to Robert.

"This what you wanted?" His tone is controlled as he fucks me like he's trying to break me. "You come here to lose thousands of dollars so someone will fuck you and use you?"

"Yes." The word is muffled against his palm.

"Say it again."

"Yes. Please. I wanted this."

"Wanted what? Be specific."

My mind scrambles for words. "I wanted to be used. Wanted someone to look at me and see—" I gasp as he hits a spot that whites out my vision. "See what I really—"

"What?"

"A whore." The confession tears out of me in fragments. "A bored—hungry—slut who can't stop—" Another deep plunge almost makes me lose the thread.

"—thinking about this. About being fucked by men who aren't—oh god."

The pleasure builds and my thighs are shaking. My nails scrape against concrete. My whole body is straining toward the edge.

Adrian pulls out.

I make a sound I don't recognize. Half sob, half animal. I rock backward, but there's nothing there.

"Turn around. Get on your knees."

I turn. My legs almost give out, and I sink to the floor awkwardly in my heels. The concrete bites into my knees, and I look up at him.

He's stroking himself slowly. Watching me with that assessing expression.

"Open your mouth."

I do. Wider than I need to. My tongue is out, waiting. I close my eyes instinctively.

I hear the wet sound of him speeding up his hand until he groans. Hot stripes across my cheek and lips. The warmth drips down my skin. I lick my lips, tasting salt and musk.

When I open my eyes, he's gazing down at me, an unmistakable glint of triumph in his expression as he tucks himself into his slacks and buckles his belt.

"Next time," he says calmly, "I might let you come."

He retrieves a box of tissues from a nearby shelf.

"Clean yourself up. And Shannon?" He opens the door and pauses as I blink at him. "You coming isn't a guarantee. I want you to think about that."

The door clicks shut behind him, leaving me kneeling on the storage room floor.

My clit throbs in protest of the denied orgasm. Every heartbeat makes it worse. I press my thighs together and the friction is a tease. A reminder of how close I was.

I've never been left like this. Wound tight enough to scream.

I've never been more turned on in my life.

I use the tissues to clean my face, and all I can think about is how badly I need to orgasm. Holy fuck. My body is one exposed wire, sparking at nothing.

This was probably the point.

Tony gave me what I wanted. Adrian made me want more.

Chapter 5

I take a quick trip to the bathroom before I leave, and the fluorescent light is unforgiving, the mirror showing me someone I didn't know existed. There's mascara smudged beneath my eyes. My lips are swollen. I'm flushed, and I look like exactly what I am—a woman who got fucked in a storage room and sent away unsatisfied.

I fix what I can, wetting a paper towel to scrub at my face, smoothing my hair, tugging my dress back into place.

When I'm semi-presentable I speed walk as fast as I can in these heels. All I can think about is getting home to Robert. I need my husband.

By the time I get to my car, I'm trembling so hard I can hardly unlock the door.

Once I'm inside, I pull out my phone.

SHANNON: Settled some of my tab. Tony says hi. On my way.

I stare at the message after I send it.

Tony didn't say hi. I don't even know if Adrian actually settled my debt. It doesn't matter.

Forty-two minutes until home.

I fucked two men tonight. Tony's mark is on my thigh. I missed some of the cum on my face. I can feel it dried and crusty.

As I drive, things surface. The stuff I've been pushing down since Tony's office. The photo with the state senator. Adrian walking in without knocking. Like an equal.

The conversation about suppliers. About payments. They're not just running a casino.

I don't know what they're doing, but it requires political connections and backup plans and men like Adrian who handle problems coldly and without sentiment.

Robert wouldn't want me going back if he knew. I'm certain of that. He said yes to extramarital sex, not to whatever is happening at that casino.

Part of me doesn't want to tell him at all. Because telling him might mean losing access to this. To whoever I become when I walk through those casino doors.

When I pull into our garage, I don't know what I'm going to do. Well, what I'm going to do after I get my husband's cock inside me. That's the priority.

Robert is waiting in the bedroom.

He's sitting on the edge of the bed in sweatpants and nothing else. When I walk in, his gaze rakes over me. The smeared makeup. The wrinkled dress. The way I'm fighting to hold myself together.

"Shannon." He's on his feet, crossing to me in two strides. One hand grasps my waist and the other cups my face, tilting my chin up. "Are you okay?"

"Yes." My voice cracks. "No. I don't know."

"Tell me."

I give him the highlights of Tony's office, and Robert's breathing speeds up. His hold on my waist goes rigid.

I tell him about the poker table. The reckless bets. The thousands I threw away because I was chasing a high.

"What happened then?" His words come out rough.

I tell him about Adrian. The storage room. About how close I was when Adrian pulled out and finished on my face.

"He didn't let you come?"

"No." My face burns. "He said next time he might."

He groans, but I catch a flicker of something on his face. The corner of his mouth lifts like he's won something.

"You let another man edge you."

"I..." My throat tightens. "It's not like I asked for it."

Robert laughs. "Shannon, you said he left you there. You could have finished yourself."

He's right.

"You came home to me instead."

"Yes."

He backs me up until I'm flush against the nearest wall. "That's everything I wanted."

My breath catches and a fresh wave of arousal makes my body respond.

"Show me." His fingers slide into my hair. "Show me how he fucked you."

I spin until I'm facing the wall and rest my palms on the plaster.

Our bedroom wall is smooth, not cold concrete. And Robert knows how to touch me in ways Adrian never will. He knows how to angle my hips to hit the spot that makes me come hard every time.

"He touched you here?" Robert cups me through the fabric of my panties, soaked through, and I whimper.

"Yes. But he was rougher. He didn't care about..."

"About what you needed." Robert pulls my panties down to my knees and rubs my clit with the skill of a man who's spent fifteen years learning my body. "He took what he wanted and left you aching."

"Yes." I'm trembling. Close enough that I might come before he even fucks me. The orgasm I was denied is right there, and Robert knows it.

"Look at you." There's wonder in his voice. "So wound up you can barely stand. Another man did this to you and sent you home to me."

He spins me around, yanks his sweatpants down, and lifts me against the wall. He pushes inside me in one smooth stroke.

I cry out. The stretch is different, but just as wonderful.

"Beg for it." Robert's words are rough as he fucks me.

Fuuuck. The words stream out of my mouth. "Please, Robert. Please. I need to come. He didn't let me and I... please..."

"That's it." He slides his hand between us and circles my clit while he hammers me into the wall.

My orgasm hits and I scream. My body convulses around him, voice cracking. Robert holds me pinned to the wall, fucking me through it, his own groans mixing with mine.

"Again," he says.

He carries me to the bed. Bends me over the mattress the way Tony bent me over his desk. He drives into me from behind with long, deep strokes that make me sob into the bedding. He rubs my clit again, relentless, and I shatter a second time with his name tearing from my throat.

"Again."

He flips me onto my back, hooks my legs over his shoulders. Fucks me deep and hard. I'm lit up everywhere. The third orgasm crests as Robert's rhythm falters.

"Look at me." His eyes lock on mine, fierce. "You're mine, Shannon. No matter who else touches you. No matter who else makes you scream."

"Yours. Always yours."

He groans and we come at the same time. His warm cum fills me as color sparkles along the edges of my vision. Pleasure turns my mind to mush and there's nothing but the two of us as he fucks me through the ecstasy.

Afterward, we lie tangled together. The ceiling fan turns lazy circles above us. Robert's hand rests on my hip, then slides down to my thigh. His fingers move higher until they find the mark.

He goes still.

"What's this?" His voice is quiet, but there's heat underneath.

I know what he's found. Tony's hickey. Dark purple against pale skin, positioned exactly where only an intimate partner would see it.

"Tony." The word comes out breathy.

Robert's thumb presses against the bruise. I hiss at the tender sting.

"Here." His touch is possessive as he circles the mark. "On your inner thigh. Where I'd be the only one to see it when I fucked you."

"Yes."

His eyes meet mine, and that look I predicted is there—raw and claiming. *Mine.*

"He marked you for me to find." Robert's thumb presses harder, and I gasp. "Wanted me to know exactly where his mouth was on you."

"Robert—"

He shifts, pushing my thighs apart so he can see it properly. The hickey is vivid against my skin, unmistakable.

"Fuck." The word is reverent. His thumb finds another bruise—Adrian's fingerprints, forming—and moves over it slowly.

"Two men." His voice is drowsy, satisfied. "In one night."

"Three, counting you."

His snort makes me smile. "And you came home to me."

I look at him. The lines around his eyes that I've watched deepen over fifteen years. This man who asked me to explore and then turned my exploration into the fuel for our best sex in a decade.

"I'll always come home to you."

He kisses my forehead tenderly and snuggles against me again. His breathing slows, evens out, and I know he's drifting toward sleep.

I stare at the ceiling fan. I told him about every touch and every obscene word.

But I forgot to tell him about the used panties. That wasn't on purpose, and it'll probably earn me a hard fucking tomorrow when I do.

I said I'd tell him everything, but I didn't tell him what I suspect about Tony's connections. About the business that isn't the real business.

I can't—not yet. I need one more time. Then I'll come clean.

I close my eyes.

Next time, I'm not going to stumble into anything unaware.

Next time, I'm done playing it safe on the main floor. I want to know what it takes to become a high roller.

The End

About Lacey Cross

Lacey Cross is a wife sharing erotica writer with over 100 short stories published since she started in 2021. Her stories emphasize the pleasure found from the wife living her best slut life and embracing the hotwife lifestyle. She explores themes of free use, submissive wives with dominant bulls, BDSM...and oh-so-many men.